THE DUCK WHO LOST THE COURAGE TO SWIM

Believe in Yourself—Get Rid of Fear

BERNICE L. DUNLAP

This book is dedicated to
my grandchildren, Kerry, Kayla,
Alexis, Madison, and Aleah
and my s/g: Asia—
I love you all!

One Saturday morning, Snowflake went to the lake to meet Goldie Duck. When she got there, Goldie was sitting on the ground near the water. "Hi Goldie," said Snowflake, "the water looks great today! Are you ready to go swimming? "At first Goldie just rolled her eyes and turned away from Snowflake. After a few seconds, Goldie turned back around, and in an unhappy voice she said, "No, I have lost my courage to swim." Snowflakes sat down beside Goldie. "What's wrong with you?

And when did you start thinking like that?"

Goldie said, "Last night I had a bad dream. I dreamed I was swimming in the lake, and I drowned."

"But Goldie it was only a bad dream," said Snowflake.

"I know," said Goldie, "but it seems so real to me."

"Aw, come on; pull out of it, Goldie. I have never met a duck who lost their courage to swim." Snowflake put her arms around Goldie, and said, "Listen, sometimes we all have bad dreams, but when we wake up, we know they are not real, and we go on with life."

As Snowflake and Goldie were sitting near the lake and talking to each other, along hopped Buddy Rabbit. "Hello friends," said Buddy Rabbit, "Why aren't you guys swimming and enjoying the water today?"

Goldie didn't want to talk about it, but Snowflake told Buddy about Goldie's bad dream.

"I am so sorry Goldie. I wish I could help you with that. I have never met any ducks who lost their courage to swim," said Buddy Rabbit.

Either have I," said Snowflake.

"Why don't you guys ask Doctor Hoot Owl for some advice?"

"That is a great idea!' Snowflake said. Goldie and I are going to give Doctor Hoot Owl a visit today."

Okay," said Buddy Rabbit. Good luck! I will see you guys later,' and he hopped away.

After Buddy Rabbit left, Snowflake asked Goldie to go with her to find Doctor Hoot Owl. Teary-eyed, Goldie said, "No, I don't feel like it. You go on. I just want to stay here."

Snowflake waddled into the woods, where she ran in to J Wren and T Wren, the bird brothers, playing in front of their house. "Have you guys seen Doctor Hoot Owl today?" she asked.

"No, said T Wren, nobody ever sees Doctor Hoot Owl up this time of day! He sleeps during the day and comes out at night."

"We can show you where he lives,' said J Wren. "Follow us!"

Later, Snowflake saw a big tree stump, and she stopped and sat down. T Wren looked back at her and asked, "Why are you stopping?"

"Because I am tired," said Snowflake.

"But Doctor Hoot Owl's house is right over there in that big oak tree," said J Wren.

"Oh, all right, thank you guys, but I just want to rest a few minutes," said Snowflake.

"You are welcome," said T and J wren at the same time.

Well, now that you know where he lives, we are going back home...See you later; Snowflake said the Wren brothers, and they flew off.

After resting a few minutes, Snowflake got up and began to walk toward the big oak tree.

Finally, she arrived at the foot of the tree. Looking up, she stood there calling the owl's name. "Doctor Hoot, Doctor Hoot, where are you?"

Dr. Hoot Owl came out of his house shaking his feathers angrily. "What is the matter with you, coming here waking me up? He asked. Don't you know I work hard at night and I have to get my rest during the day?"

"I am very sorry, but I need some advice," said Snowflake.

"It better be good. "What is it?" said Doctor Hoot Owl.

"My friend Goldie Duck is unhappy because she lost her courage to swim."

"What?" Ducks are not supposed to lose their courage to swim."

"Exactly, Doctor. Can you help?" said Snowflake.

"Oh, all right," said Doctor Hoot Owl, "I have an idea that might work.

"Here is my advice. You and one of your friends...blindfold Goldie and then guide her into the water," and I think she will find her courage again."

Snowflake started to say thank you, but the owl had already gone back into his house to go back to sleep.

Next Snowflake headed to her friend Swayback's House and told her the whole story.

"What can I do to help?" Swayback asked.

"First, do you have something we can blindfold Goldie?" "Yes I do…I have a scarf in the closet we can use, "said Swayback. "Okay, let's grab that scarf and go to the lake." Said Snowflake.

When they got to the lake, Snowflake and Swayback convinced Goldie to let them blindfold and guide her into the water. The more Goldie swam with the support of her friends, the more she felt encouraged to swim. Then all at once, in the middle of the lake, Goldie yelled, "Let me go! I feel like I can swim now! I have found my courage again!" so they let her go.

Hey wait for us, Goldie,' said Snowflake and Swayback. Happily, giving a wing bump to each other, Snowflake and Swayback were so glad that Goldie found her courage to swim again.

So, Goldie swam with Snowflake and Swayback, splashing, kicking, and ducking their heads under the water. "I can't believe it! I love swimming now! This is the best time I ever had in this lake!" said Goldie. Snowflake and Swayback agreed.

Therefore, Goldie decided no matter what bad dreams she might have in the future... she knew that dreams are not real, and all ducks have the courage to swim.

"QUACK, QUACK, QUACK!" the three ducks shouted.

THE END